TONY'S NEW FRIEND

Karen Anne De Santis

Illustrated by Amanda Barkley

Carol, you've made a difference!

Karen Anne De Santis

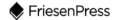 FriesenPress

Suite 300 - 990 Fort St
Victoria, BC, V8V 3K2
Canada

www.friesenpress.com

ISBN
978-1-5255-9136-5 (Hardcover)
978-1-5255-9135-8 (Paperback)
978-1-5255-9137-2 (eBook)

1. JUVENILE FICTION, FAMILY, MULTIGENERATIONAL

Distributed to the trade by The Ingram Book Company

This book is dedicated to my husband Ciro and my family for supporting me during this writing process. I also dedicate this book to my mom, Marie Ash, who lived in a retirement home and loved all the activities and social interactions that they provided.

To parents, teachers and students, let's all help our elderly citizens and visit them regularly. We can ALL benefit from intergenerational friendships.

Amanda Barkley, a creative sketch artist/illustrator, dedicates this book to her husband Mitchell and daughter, Charlotte.

Tony woke up in the morning,
ALL READY to start his day.
He put on his shirt, put on his shorts
And was ready to go out and **PLAY**.

He yelled to his mom, yelled to dad,
"WHAT SHOULD I DO FOR FUN?"
"Go outside, walk around,
Play, your day has begun!"

He walked around
the neighbourhood
Looking for James,
his friend.

MERT VILLAGE
RETIREMENT HOME

Mert Village

He looked to the right,
looked to the left
And saw a building
just round' the bend.

With a little hesitation,
He walked up to the big, glass door.
He saw some movement as he peered inside.
There were **WHEELCHAIRS** all on the floor.

"WHAT IS THIS?" he said out loud.
Surely, someone would know.
He opened the door, walked right through,
His small feet were raring to go.

He looked around the spacious room
And spotted a **LITTLE OLD MAN.**
His head was down, his eyes were closed.
There were wrinkles all over his hand.

Tony crept a little closer,
All ready to make a **NEW FRIEND**.
He touched his shoulder, held his hand,
The man **OPENED** his eyes and said:

"**HELLO**, my name is Forrest.
This is my brand new home.
Come sit with me for a while,
So I don't feel so **ALONE.**"

Tony took a chair, sat right down
And soon began to speak.
"I can be your **NEW FRIEND**, Forrest.
I just live right down the street!"

Forrest told Tony about his **PAST**
And the life that he used to live.
He shared his story of days gone by.
He had **SO** much more to give.

The two friends talked for hours,
Excitement was in their eyes.
There was no judgment, no holding back.
Their friendship was a **BIG SURPRISE.**

It was time for Tony to walk on home,
The morning had come to an **END.**
Forrest had to go back to his room.
He was **PROUD** to have made a new friend.

Tony had helped him **REMEMBER**
Of time that had passed on by.
He gave him a hug, a squeeze of the hand.
They both had a **TWINKLE** in their eye.

As Tony walked home,
back down the street,
He thought of his **WONDERFUL** day.
It doesn't matter how old you are,
"MAKE A DIFFERENCE!"
is what I will say.

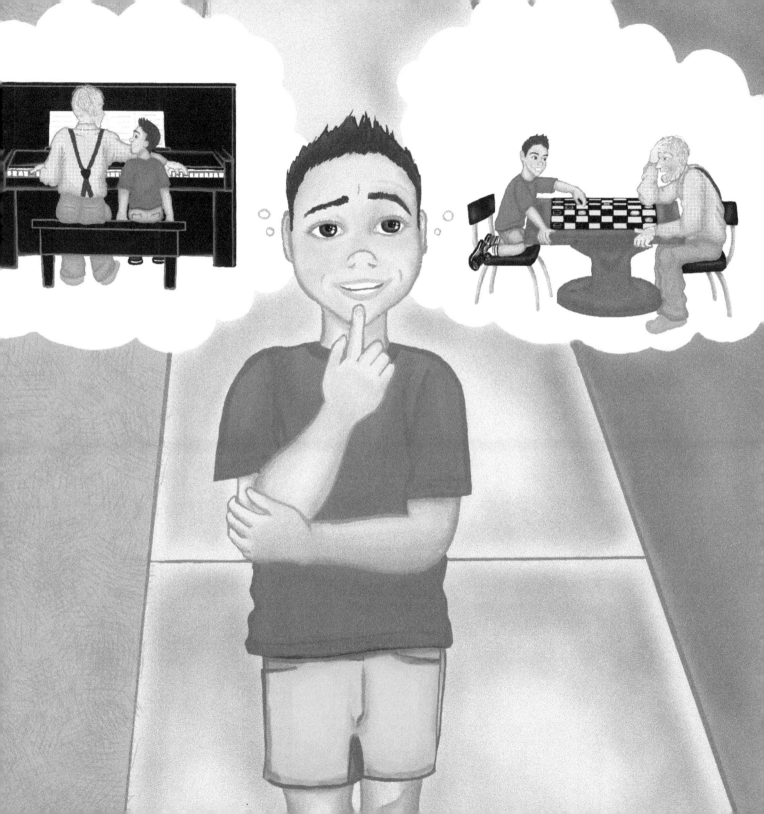

Tony tossed and turned and thought all night,
He **COULDN'T WAIT** to share with his school.
He had to tell his teacher, his friends.
It was the best idea... **SO COOL!!**

"We have to **VISIT** an old age home,
There are people who are in need.
They have to talk, they need to share,
Let's **ALL** do this very **GOOD** deed."

So once a month, Tony's **WHOLE** class
Visits a retirement place.
They do arts and crafts, sing some songs,
A **SMILE** on everyone's face.

Friendships are made, bonds are formed
And the young and the old agree.
Making a difference in someone's life
**IS IMPORTANT TO
YOU AND ME!**

www.ingramcontent.com/pod-product-compliance
Lightning Source LLC
Jackson TN
JSHW072244230225
79416JS00009B/24